Fast Fox and Slow Snail

'Fast Fox and Slow Snail'
An original concept by Lou Treleaven
© Lou Treleaven

Illustrated by David Creighton-Pester

Published by MAVERICK ARTS PUBLISHING LTD

Studio 3A, City Business Centre, 6 Brighton Road,

Horsham, West Sussex, RH13 5BB

© Maverick Arts Publishing Limited July 2017

+44 (0)1403 256941

ISBN 978-1-84886-295-1

Maverick
arts publishing
www.maverickbooks.co.uk

This book is rated as: Blue Band (Guided Reading)
This story is decodable at Letters and Sounds Phase 4.

Fast Fox and Slow Snail

by Lou Treleaven

illustrated by
David Creighton-Pester

Fast Fox likes to go fast.

Slow Snail likes to go slow.

"Let's go for a walk in the woods,"
says Slow Snail.

"I never walk, I run," says Fast Fox.

Fast Fox runs off to the woods.

Slow Snail creeps along.

Slow Snail is not lost.

He is looking at a flower.

Fast Fox is still running.

She looks for Slow Snail.

She cannot see the flower.

Slow Snail spots a bee.

Hello, Buzzy Bee.

Fast Fox is still running.

She cannot see Slow Snail.

She cannot see the bee.

Where is that Slow Snail?

Slow Snail creeps along a log.

It is brown with soft green moss.

Fast Fox sees Slow Snail.

She stops.

Fast Fox sees the flower,

the bee and the log.

Fast Fox walks along the log.

"This is fun," says Fast Fox.

"Yes," says Slow Snail.

"I never run, I walk."

"Good," says Fast Fox.

Quiz

1. What does Fast Fox never do?
a) Walk
b) Run
c) Hop

2. What is Slow Snail looking at?
a) A fox
b) A wood
c) A flower

3. What does the bee say?
a) Goodbye, Slow Snail
b) Hello, Slow Snail
c) How do you do, Fast Fox

4. Where does Fast Fox find Slow Snail?
a) In a tree
b) On a log
c) In a pond

5. "Let's go _____"?
a) Slow
b) Fast
c) Run

Turn over for answers

Book Bands for Guided Reading

The Institute of Education book banding system is a scale of colours that reflects the various levels of reading difficulty. The bands are assigned by taking into account the content, the language style, the layout and phonics.

Maverick Early Readers are a bright, attractive range of books covering the pink to purple bands. All of these books have been book banded for guided reading to the industry standard and edited by a leading educational consultant.

For more titles visit:
www.maverickbooks.co.uk/early-readers

 Pink

 Red

 Yellow

 Blue

 Green

 Orange

 Turquoise

 Purple

 Book Band Blue

Fast Fox and Slow Snail	978-1-84886-295-1
Mine, Mine, Mine Said the Porcupine	978-1-84886-296-8
The Smart Hat	978-1-84886-294-4
Strictly No Crocs	978-1-84886-240-1
Bibble and the Bubbles	978-1-84886-224-1

Quiz Answers: 1a, 2c, 3b, 4b, 5a